For Kaitlyn and Tara, with Father Kisses!

—D. R.

For Scott, my handsome prince, with love and kisses.

—L. R.

kiss, _n._ a caress with the lips.
kissable, _adj._ someone or
something worthy of kissing.
Ant unkissable

A Book of
Kisses

by Dave Ross
illustrated by Laura Rader

HARPERCOLLINSPUBLISHERS

Library of Congress Cataloging-in-Publication Data
Ross, Dave, 1949–
    A book of kisses / by Dave Ross ; illustrated by Laura Rader.
        p.   cm.
    Summary: Describes all the different types of kisses there are for all different occasions
including butterfly kisses, tiptoe kisses, and "Ew Yuck!" kisses.
    ISBN 0-06-028169-3. — ISBN 0-06-028453-6 (lib. bdg.)
    [1. Kissing—Fiction.]   I. Rader, Laura, ill.   II. Title.
PZ7.R71964Br   2000   98-49562
[E]—dc21   CIP
                                                                        AC

Typography by Al Cetta   1   2   3   4   5   6   7   8   9   10   ❖   First Edition

There are all kinds of kisses in the world . . .

Good Morning Kisses

Going to School Kisses
Sometimes this is called the Kiss-and-Go.

After School Kisses

Sometimes a kiss is better than a snack.

When Mom or Dad Comes Home Kisses

Good Night Kisses

Lots of families also have Getting-into-Bed Kisses,

Bedtime Story Kisses,
and
Turning-Out-the-Light
Kisses.

There are kisses for when you come and go.
Hello Kisses

Good-bye Kisses
In some countries, these are Double Cheek Kisses.

Bon Voyage Kisses

Wave from the Car Kisses
Also known as Smeary Window Kisses.

There are kisses that make you feel better.

Boo-boo Kisses

Sick-in-Bed Kisses
Sometimes these lead
to
Doctor Visit Kisses.

I'm Sorry Kisses

Often the best way to end an argument is with a kiss.

But a handshake will do, too!

There are kisses for special occasions.

Good Report Card Kisses

Winning Kisses

Congratulations Kisses

Valentine Kisses

Birthday Kisses

These only come around once a year,
so make the most of them!

And, of course, there are Family Kisses.

Sometimes called an Assembly Line Kiss in large families.

Family Kisses include:
Mom and Dad Kisses

Grandma and Grandpa Kisses

Great-Uncle Fred Kisses
Watch out for the whiskers!

Yuck!

Brother and Sister Kisses
Otherwise known as "Ew Yuck!" Kisses.

Short or tall, near or far, there are as many ways of kissing as there are different kinds of people.

Promise Kisses

First make a promise.

Then kiss your pinky.

Touch pinkies.

Now you've made a promise kiss!

Just remember to keep it.

Tiptoe Kisses
Useful for small children.

Forehead Kisses
  Used frequently by tall people.

Nose and Toes Kisses

Tummy Kisses

Sometimes called a Raspberry Kiss.

Butterfly Kisses

Bat your eyelashes against someone's cheek—that's a Butterfly Kiss!

Underwater Kisses

Remember to breathe out!

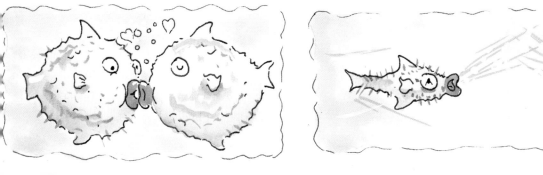

Rubbing Noses Kisses

These can keep you warm on cold days!

Bubble Gum Kisses

Caution, you can get stuck on these kisses.

Candy Kisses
are very sweet.

Princess Kisses

Perfect for greeting a princess, but not very nice
if her hands are unwashed!

Prince Kisses

You may have to kiss a lot of frogs

before you find the handsome prince.

Across the Room Kisses

Kiss your hand. Then throw the kiss.
Throw it well so you don't miss!

Telephone Kisses

Letter Kisses

A kiss is an easy way
to remind someone you care.

Kisses can be given
anytime, anywhere.

If kisses are given with love and respect,
they turn a rotten day into a great day.

All kisses say special things,

You're special. I love you.

but the most special
thing a kiss can say
is "I Love You."